Redworld is published by
Stone Arch Books, A Capstone Imprint
1710 Roe Crest Drive
North Mankato, Minnesota 56003
www.mycapstone.com

Library of Congress Cataloging-in-Publication Data
Names: Collins, A. L. (Ai Lynn), 1964- author. | Tikulin, Tomislav, illustrator.
Title: Legacy : relics of Mars / by A. L. Collins ; illustrated by Tomislav Tikulin.
Description: North Mankato, Minnesota : Stone Arch Books, a Capstone imprint, [2018] |
    Series: Sci-finity. Redworld ; [4]
Summary: Now in seventh grade, Belle Song has settled into her life on Mars; she has a new
    baby sister, her android Melody, her wolf-dog Raider, and her friends, the half-alien Lucas,
    and the Nabian, Ta'al. But when she and Ta'al uncover some ancient ruins, which the Nabians
    claim are a sacred site, Belle finds herself plunged into a tricky world of extraterrestrial
    politics and religion that threatens her relationship with Ta'al.
Identifiers: LCCN 2017002462 (print) | LCCN 2017008292 (ebook) |
    ISBN 9781496548221 (library binding) | ISBN 9781496548344 (eBook PDF)
Subjects: LCSH: Antiquities—Juvenile fiction. | Extraterrestrial beings—Juvenile fiction. |
    Friendship—Juvenile fiction. | Interpersonal relations—Juvenile fiction. | Farm life—Juvenile
    fiction. | Families—Juvenile fiction. | Science fiction. | Mars (Planet)—Juvenile fiction. |
    CYAC: Science fiction. | Antiquities—Fiction. | Human-alien encounters—Fiction. |
    Friendship—Fiction. | Interpersonal relations—Fiction. | Farm life—Fiction. | Family life—
    Fiction. | Mars (Planet)—Fiction. | LCGFT: Science fiction.
Classification: LCC PZ7.1.C6447 Le 2018 (print) | LCC PZ7.1.C6447 (ebook) |
    DDC 813.6 [Fic]—dc23
LC record available at https://lccn.loc.gov/2017002462

Editor: Aaron J. Sautter
Designer: Ted Williams
Production: Kathy McColley

Printed and bound in Canada.
010382F17

BY A.L. COLLINS
ILLUSTRATED BY TOMISLAV TIKULIN

STONE ARCH BOOKS
a capstone imprint

MT. OLYMPUS
(RESERVOIR)
MT.
ASCREUS
MT.
PAVONIS
MT.
ARSIA
SIRENUM ROAD
BARREN
LANDS
CITIES
ROADS
MOUNTAINS
FOREST
DESALINATION
PLANTS
FARMS
ABANDONED
FARMS

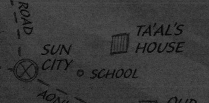

OLYMPIA PROVINCE

THARSIS CITY ⊗

FERRY LANDING

N
W — E
S

MARINE VALLEY RIVER

SUN VALLEY ROAD

TA'AL'S HOUSE

SUN CITY ⊗
○ SCHOOL

AONIA ROAD

OUR FARM

WALKER FARM

RAIDERS!

DARWIN CITY

Belle Song

Thirteen-year-old Belle can be headstrong and stubborn. Her curiosity and sense of adventure often get her into trouble. Still, she has a good heart and is passionate about fairness. She is fiercely loyal to her friends.

Yun and Zara Song

Belle's parents sometimes seem really strict. But Yun has a great sense of humor, which Belle both loves and is embarrassed by. Zara has a generous heart, which has taught Belle not to judge others too quickly.

Melody

Melody is an old model 3X Personal Home Helper android. She was given to Belle by her grandmother before she passed away. Melody is Belle's best friend and protector and enjoys telling bad jokes to seem more human.

MAIN INHABITANTS

Lucas Walker

Lucas is Belle's neighbor and classmate. He is part Sulux and part human. Meeting new people is not easy for him. But once he knows someone, his adventurous side emerges. He is full of ideas, which sometimes gets him and his friends into trouble.

Ta'al

Ta'al and her family are Nabian, an ancient alien race from another star system. Born and raised on Mars, Ta'al is intelligent and curious. She enjoys exploring and adventure and quickly becomes Belle's closest friend on Mars.

Raider

Raider is a hybrid wolf-dog. These animals were bred to be tame pets, but some of them became wild. After Raider is rescued by Belle, he becomes a faithful and protective companion.

It is the year 2335. Life on Earth is very difficult. Widespread disease, a lack of resources, and a long war against intelligent robots has caused much suffering. Some Terrans, those who are from Earth, have moved to the Lunar Colony in search of a better life. But the Moon is overcrowded and has limited resources. Other families have chosen to move to Mars instead. With the help of two alien races — the Sulux and the Nabians — the red planet was transformed to support life nearly 200 years ago.

Yun and Zara Song and their daughter, Belle, moved to Mars a year ago to get a fresh start in life. Here they live as farmers. They work hard to grow crops and raise hybrid animals that are suitable for life on Mars.

The Songs have survived many hardships while learning to live on Mars. The move was especially hard on Belle. She hated Mars at first. But over time she learned to appreciate the red planet, and she's made several friends along the way. However, when Belle accidentally makes an incredible discovery, it creates some serious tensions and arguments between her friends and the different races of . . .

CHAPTER ONE
:NEW ARRIVALS:

Summertime on Mars was the best time of year. The
weather was perfect and warm. The sky was a constant clear
blue, with only the occasional puffy cloud floating by. Even
the dust storms, famous for ruining Martians' outdoor lives,
were nowhere to be seen. Belle didn't even mind being in
school twice a week.

"I'm secretly glad all of your parents had to go away this
week," Belle said to her best friend, Taal. Taal was Nabian,

and unlike human children, she had three parents. "I've been dying for some real conversation. All anyone talks about around here is the baby."

Ta'al carried Thea, Belle's baby sister, in her arms. Belle's mom, Zara, had given birth a few months before. Belle had been her mom's primary helper ever since. Meanwhile, Belle's dad, Yun, and her android, Melody, tended to the farm. Belle loved Thea. However, she didn't want to say it out loud: but she'd grown rather sick of her baby sister.

Ta'al rocked back and forth on her feet, cooing at the tiny girl, who gurgled contentedly.

"I'd never be tired of this little darling," Ta'al said. She smiled at Belle, who wrinkled her nose as if the baby smelled bad. "But I'm glad to be staying with you this week too. I would have loved to go to Lunar Colony with my parents, but they didn't want me to miss school."

"Well, the results of the Olympia Schools Science Fair will be out soon," Belle said. "If we win, we'll get to go to Tharsis City for the finals. That'll be exciting."

"Only if we win," Ta'al said. She and Belle had worked all winter and spring on improving Belle's Petripuffs. The palm-sized balls were an effective defensive weapon. When thrown at an attacker, the puffs released a paralyzing powder, giving the thrower enough time to get away.

"Yeah, you and I might win instead, Belle." Lucas Walker bounced into the living room. Lucas was Belle's neighbor and other science fair partner. They'd been working on a different project to create a new feed formula for growing turken chicks bigger and faster than feeding them the usual grains. The ugly half-turkey, half-chicken birds were an important food source for most farmers.

"How did you get in so quietly?" Belle hadn't even heard Lucas arrive.

"My mother says I have to be extra quiet with the baby around," Lucas said, peeking at Thea in Ta'al's arms. "That's a tall order for me. Ha!" He let out a loud chortle, then immediately slapped his hand over his mouth. "Oops, sorry."

Belle jumped up out of her seat. "I need to get outside," she said, pointing to the wallscreen that projected the above-ground scene. The climate on Mars could often be extreme. Winters were brutally cold, and fierce dust storms often swept across the Martian plains. Because of this, most Martian homes were built underground for protection. But some days, like today, the weather could be perfect.

"We can't stay below on a beautiful, sunny day like this," Belle concluded.

Ta'al had managed to put Thea to sleep. She gently placed the baby back into her rocking crib. A mechanism inside sensed the baby's presence and a blanket gently wrapped itself around her little body like a cocoon. The baby sighed happily and went to sleep. An invisible barrier, similar to a force field, formed around her crib like a bubble. It shielded the baby from loud noises and purified her breathing air. This device had been a gift from Ta'al's family. It used special Nabian technology.

The others could now speak with normal voices without worrying about waking up the baby. Lucas shook himself, as if he'd been restraining himself the whole time. Belle had to laugh. Her friend reminded her of Raider, her hybrid wolf-dog pet.

"My mom tells me we have new neighbors," Lucas said.

"Yes," Ta'al confirmed. "The Parks have retired and moved to Utopia. They sold their farm to a new family."

Utopia was on the other side Mars. Belle had been there only once before, when her family had first moved to the red planet. She remembered it being very dusty. She couldn't imagine why Mr. and Mrs. Park would want to retire there.

"Then let's go see if the new neighbors have kids," Belle said. She went to tell her mom that they were leaving.

"Stay out of trouble," Zara said as they ran up the stairs to the above-ground portion of their home. "And don't forget to feed the dog!"

Raider met them at the top of the stairs. He wagged his huge tail and perked up his ears. He licked Belle's hand and then looked to Ta'al to be petted. Ta'al tapped his head once and moved away. Most Nabians didn't really like pets. Raider nudged Lucas' hand instead, knowing that this friend would give him what he wanted. Lucas loved animals.

The three friends raced across the back of Belle's family farm and ran into her dad. Yun and Melody were making repairs to some posts that had been damaged by a dust storm at the end of spring. Raider jumped up on Melody and licked her face. He had always liked the android. Melody petted him in return. As Ta'al and Lucas ran on, Belle told Yun where they were headed. She hoped her dad wouldn't give her a long lecture about how she seemed to get into trouble whenever she went off on her own.

"Do you promise not to get into mischief?" he asked, narrowing his eyes.

"We're only going to see if we'll have new classmates at school next week," she said. "And to be neighborly." She gave him her best pleading face. Even Raider whined a little, as if he understood what was going on.

"I believe the family does have children," Yun said. "They were mentioned at the parents' meeting last night."

"Then it's only polite to go and say hello." Belle remembered how Lucas' family had welcomed them when they first arrived. She hadn't appreciated it at the time. But later she realized she was glad to have met at least one person her own age before school started.

"Don't be back too late," Yun said. "And remember, stay out of trouble."

Belle ran to catch up with her friends. Raider trotted at her side. The three friends climbed over the back gate and headed north along the dirt path that ran among the different farms. They ran past the Walker farm, and another unoccupied farm. Eventually they found themselves among tall, green hedges that formed a wall around the Parks' old farm. Belle felt as if she were in a giant maze.

"There it is!" Lucas said, pointing to the house in the middle of several corrals. Just like Belle's family house, this one was a little run down. But many Martian families didn't really keep their above-ground houses in good shape. There wasn't much point, really, since they lived most of the year below ground.

"Let's go and introduce ourselves," Belle said.

Ta'al fell behind them as they ran ahead. Raider stopped to wait for her.

"Come on," Belle called.

"What if they don't like Nabians?" Ta'al spoke hesitantly.

When Belle had first moved to Mars, she noticed that some people were rude to Nabians. In fact, Lucas had been one of them at first. Belle had learned that Nabians and Sulux had a shared history of resentment. About two hundred years ago, their people argued over whether or not to help humans terraform Mars. The Nabians felt that humans weren't ready for advanced technology. But the Sulux, who were eager to share Mars with the humans, simply gave it to them. It was Sulux technology that allowed Mars to be terraformed and made livable. The bitterness between the two peoples was never really resolved. Some Sulux still disliked Nabians, which meant that some humans did too. Ta'al and her family had firsthand experience with the prejudices of these people.

"Hey, you got me to like you," Lucas said with a grin. "Don't worry. We won't let anyone be mean to you."

Ta'al laughed. Together, they approached the computer panel at the side of the house door. Belle took a deep breath and pressed the intercom button.

Sol 91/Summer, Mars Cycle 106

Our new neighbors are the Senn family. They have three kids — twin boys and a girl. The twins, Alex and Aiden, are a year older than us. The girl is our age. Her name is Ava. She wasn't home when we went to say hello. Alex and Aiden are great. They're funny, like Lucas. And they're Terran, just like me. They moved here from Earth last week and are still trying to get used to things here, like the gravity, and the hybrid animals, and the weird food we eat.

Actually, it sounds pretty familiar to what I first went through. It's funny. I've been here just over a year, but I feel like I'm as Martian as anyone else. I don't have the red rings in my eyes like Thea does. That's because she was born on Mars. But I feel Martian. I don't remember exactly when I started feeling like this place is home, but it is now.

Anyway, I understand how the Senns feel. I invited them to walk with us to school tomorrow. Ava will be with them too. Since she's thirteen, she'll be in our class with Ms. Polley. (I can't believe our 6th grade teacher moved up with us to 7th grade!) I can't wait to have another new friend.

CHAPTER TWO

BACK TO SCHOOL

The next day was a scheduled rain day. Summer was the only season warm enough to have rain on Mars. Here in Sun City it usually rained once per week, and it lasted two days. When the Sidas helped terraform Mars, their technology allowed for the creation of a specific water cycle. Rainfall was considered essential for human life to flourish, so it was made a regular part of life on the red planet.

Belle loved the rainy days. It made everything seem so fresh and clean. She would have happily run through the rain to get to school. But her mom insisted that she wear her rain gear that morning.

"It's only just starting, but I want you to stay dry. Hopefully you'll be in class before it starts to rain hard," Zara said. She adjusted Belle's hood and then pressed the knob at the end of her sleeve. The entire raincoat sealed itself snugly around Belle's body from head to toe. She would be as dry as Mars dust when she arrived at school.

Belle kissed her baby sister goodbye. Thea's skin was so soft, and she smelled kind of sweet. The baby kicked her legs in the air and gave Belle a big, toothless grin. Sometimes, Thea really was fun to have around.

Raider trotted alongside Belle until she met up with Lucas on the path behind their farms. Then the wolf-dog ran back home where he'd spend the day in the stable with their horsel, Loki. Further down the road, Ta'al joined Belle and Lucas. They chatted about their homework until they came across the Senn twins. Aiden and Alex were walking under a large umbrella. Ava was with them too, staying dry by squeezing between her brothers. She was shorter than the boys, but she had the same bright eyes. Her long, dark hair was in two braids that almost reached her hips.

Belle introduced herself and Ta'al to Ava. She greeted them with a nod, but said nothing. However, when her eyes landed on Lucas, she smiled and became quite chatty.

"What strange raincoats you have," she said, walking straight up to Lucas and running her hand along his sealed arm. Her brothers followed closely behind to keep them all under the umbrella. Lucas looked as if he was having an allergic reaction.

"You can get them in Sun City," Belle offered, staring at the new girl. "They're much more efficient than umbrellas."

"Uh-huh," Ava mumbled. She didn't even look at Belle. She was looking intently at Lucas, who was turning as red as his raingear.

Belle had a strange feeling about this girl. She looked over at Ta'al. Her friend's eyes were wide, and she had the oddest smile on her face, like she knew something that Belle didn't.

"We haven't had time to do much shopping," explained one of the twins. Belle still couldn't work out which boy was which.

"We'll probably go tomorrow," said the other.

"It might be best to wait until after the rain days are over." Ta'al pointed to the gathering clouds. "Then the roads won't be so muddy."

The new friends trudged through the increasingly heavy rain until they reached the low gray building at the edge of Sun City. The building held their school, the community center, the library, and the local medical center. Kids went to school only twice a week on Mars, so only middle schoolers were present on this day. They alternated with the elementary and high schoolers. This way, there wasn't much need for a large building.

"Welcome to Sun City School," Belle said to the Senns as they walked through the front door. Lucas ran off ahead of them. Belle and Ta'al took the Senns to the front office. There they received all the information and computer programs they would need to do their school work from home as needed. As Belle had guessed, the twins were assigned to Mr. LeCoq's eighth-grade classroom, and Ava was put into Ms. Polley's class.

"There are so few kids in our class," Ava said, when she walked into room number one and saw that there were only eight desks. "Back on Earth, I had more than thirty kids in my class."

Ava stared at the wallscreen displays, which were changing to match the age of the students occupying the room. Next, she examined the layout of the furniture.

Ms. Polley had paired the desks in a semi-circle facing the active holo-board, which displayed a holographic map of the school.

Ava turned to Belle. "Where do you sit?" she asked.

Belle pointed to the middle pair of desks. "Ta'al and I sit there."

"Where does Lucas sit?" she asked.

"At the far left," Belle said.

Belle was about to explain that Ms. Polley would assign Ava to a seat. But then Ava marched to the desk next to where Lucas would be and put her bag down.

"That's Brill's desk," Ta'al told her, as the rest of their classmates filed in. Pavish, Trina, and Brill walked in with Lucas. They were laughing over some joke Pavish had told.

Brill tried to tell Ava that she was in his seat. But Ava didn't seem to care.

"I like this desk," she said. "And since I'm new here, I'd think you'd want to be more welcoming."

Belle rolled her eyes at Ta'al who stifled a giggle. The other students simply stared at the new girl in stunned silence. Lucas tucked his head down and slipped quietly into his seat. His usual light purple half-Sulux skin had blotches of red everywhere.

When Ms. Polley entered to begin lessons, Ava went up to her and they spoke quietly for a long time. Belle strained her ears, but she couldn't hear what excuse Ava had created to pick whatever seat she wanted.

"Ava will sit with Lucas until she catches up with our work," Ms. Polley explained to the class. "Thank you, Brill, for being so generous and giving up your seat."

Brill's face went all red, and he looked really confused.

"I don't know what to think of this new girl," Belle whispered to Ta'al.

"I think she has a crush on Lucas," Ta'al said with a grin. "And she's probably used to getting whatever she wants."

Belle watched Ava during most of Agriculture lessons. She did look at Lucas an awful lot. Belle couldn't quite figure out why Ava was so interested in Lucas, with his messy hair and crooked teeth. She just didn't get it.

"I will be announcing the winners of the Science Fair on our next class day," Ms. Polley said right before lunch.

Belle and Ta'al sighed. It was hard to wait for the results.

"It's a difficult decision," Ms. Polley continued. "So many of the projects submitted are wonderful. The judges need a bit more time."

At lunch, Ava followed Lucas everywhere. She sat by him while they ate. Then she insisted on playing on his low-gravity disc team in the gym afterward. Lucas never voiced his opinion. He just kept turning darker shades of red and doing as she asked.

When Ava went to the bathroom, Belle finally got a chance to talk to Lucas. "Why don't you just tell her to leave you alone?"

"That would be rude," he said.

"You had no problem with being rude to me when we first met," Belle said. "Or with Ta'al either, for that matter."

"Ava's different," he said, chewing slowly on his snack of fried mealworms. "She's . . . very insistent."

Belle laughed. "She scares you, doesn't she?"

Lucas nodded. He slurped down his last mealworm just as Ava returned to his side.

As the school day wore on, Belle felt more and more annoyed with the new girl. She couldn't really understand why Ava irritated her. Maybe it was the way she stuck to Lucas and made him feel scared of her. Maybe it was because Ava barely spoke to Belle, except to ask about Lucas. Even more irritating was how Ava completely ignored Ta'al. She wouldn't even make eye contact with her. By the end of the school day, Belle had had enough of Ava Senn.

But Ava didn't seem to care one bit. The rain had slowed by the end of the day, so Ava and her brothers were able to

walk home without their umbrella. This allowed Ava
to walk next to Lucas. Belle couldn't believe how Ava kept
asking him stupid questions. Then, when her brothers
tried to join in the conversation, she ordered them to run
on ahead . . . and they obeyed!

Belle rolled her eyes again and turned to Ta'al.

"I forgot," she said loudly to everyone. "I need to pick
up some supplies in Sun City. Will you come with me,
Ta'al?" She pulled her friend off on a different path, in the
direction of the city center.

"What do you have to buy?" Ta'al asked when they
were alone.

"Nothing," Belle said. "I just needed to get away from
what was going on there." She pointed back toward Lucas
and Ava. They didn't even notice that the girls had left.

Belle and Ta'al walked through Sun City in silence.
Belle brooded in her own thoughts and didn't pay
attention to where she was heading. Ta'al just walked
quietly by her side, giving Belle time with her thoughts.
Soon, they were leaving the outskirts on the other side
of the city. They headed southwest, taking a path they'd
never taken before.

Belle and Ta'al walked for a while more before Ta'al
finally broke the silence.

"Why does she annoy you so much?" Ta'al asked.

"Because she makes it so obvious that she likes Lucas and no one else," Belle replied.

"I think it's funny," Ta'al replied. "Lucas is so embarrassed by the attention."

"Exactly!" Belle tried not to shout. "She's bullying him into hanging out with her."

"Oh, I don't think he minds too much." Ta'al laughed. Then she stopped and stared at Belle. "Wait, don't tell me that you're jealous!"

"Eew, no way!" Belle protested.

They kept walking. Belle was still deep in thought. *Was she jealous of Ava?* But that would mean she liked Lucas too. No. She liked him as a friend, that's all. She just didn't think anyone should monopolize her friend. Yes, that's why Ava annoyed her.

The rain had stopped for the day, and the clouds parted to reveal the bright sunlight. They continued on their path and Belle tried to talk about things other than Ava and Lucas.

"Where are we?" Belle said, suddenly looking at the strange terrain. "We've never been so far out here."

They had left the small town behind them. Laid out before them, all the way to the horizon, was flat, barren land. There were clumps of prickly bushes scattered about, but the ground was mostly rocky and dry, even though it had rained all day. It was very quiet too. Nothing seemed to live out here, for as far as their eyes could see.

"Facing this way, you'd never guess there was lush farmland nearby," Belle said. She shielded her eyes with her hand. The heat from the ground was making the air wavy. "Terraforming creates such odd spaces."

"It looks like terraforming missed this area altogether. Let's explore a bit more before heading back," Ta'al said. "I'd like to record some of this area for study." She pulled out the palm-sized disc that served as her communication device. It doubled as a recording device too. She let it scan the area as they walked along.

"Ta'al, I've been thinking about what you said." Belle watched as Ta'al gathered data of the area. "I think you're wrong about me and Lucas."

Ta'al laughed. "Are you sure?"

Belle opened her mouth to protest. But suddenly the ground beneath her feet shifted. Before she could say another word, the ground opened up and swallowed her!

CHAPTER THREE
:TRAPPED!:

"Belle! Are you all right?"

Leah's shrill scream echoed all the way down the hole to
Belle. She sounded so far away. Belle opened her eyes, but
couldn't see anything. It was completely dark. She patted the
ground around her. It was rocky, sandy, and dry. She rubbed
her arms and torso. Luckily, her clothes had protected her
from being scratched up.

What had just happened? All Belle knew was that one second she was talking to Ta'al, and then she was falling. It felt like the longest drop ever. As she fell, the rough, dry ground clawed at her until she landed with a bump at — wherever she was. It was so dark, she couldn't tell.

Belle pressed the button on her sleeve and her raingear loosened around her body. She stuck her hand under the stiff fabric and rubbed her skin. She didn't feel any blood oozing. That was good. She sat up. Her back ached and her legs hurt. She felt inside her pant leg, but again she felt no blood.

"I can't see anything," Belle cried out. Her voice bounced off the walls. *I must have fallen into some kind of well,* she thought. *Did they have wells out here?* "Ta'al, can you see me?" she called.

Ta'al was whimpering. That didn't make Belle feel better.

"Ta'al!" She needed her friend's usual calmness, or she would panic too. "Can you see me?"

"No," Ta'al called back. "This looks like some kind of shaft. It's narrow and deep."

Belle could hear Ta'al shuffling around above ground. "Can you climb up?" she called.

Belle got down on her belly and crawled toward Ta'al's voice. The ground rose sharply beneath her. She made some progress but then slid back down again.

"It's too steep," she called up, rubbing her sore hands together. "And I can't see anything."

"I'm trying to call for help, but my comm device says we're out of range," Ta'al said.

How had they walked so far out without even realizing it? The whole Ava situation must have really distracted them.

"Wait!" Ta'al sounded like she had an idea. "My comm disc! It also works as a flashlight. I could throw it to you."

"But we need it to call for help," Belle said.

"It doesn't work out here. So you might as well use it. Can you see my light?"

Belle looked up. All she saw was darkness.

"I don't think the shaft goes straight down," Belle said. "Are you shining your light now?"

"I'm going to throw my comm disc to you," Ta'al said.

"Wait," Belle replied, but it was too late. She heard the clunking of the disc as it rolled through the shaft. She waited. Seconds passed but still there was no sign of light. She closed her eyes and took deep breaths. She felt her heart pound in her chest. This was no time to cry or to panic. She had to find a way out. Fast.

She opened her eyes, and there was a sliver of light on the ground.

"I got it!" she cried. "Thank you, Ta'al."

Belle gripped the comm device and shined the light over herself first. She'd been right. She had no big cuts and barely any scratches. Her raingear had served her well.

Belle swept the light around her. She was definitely in some sort of underground shaft or well. It wasn't very big, just wide enough for her to stretch out her arms and touch the sides. The top of the shaft was not straight up. It curved away so that Belle couldn't see the surface.

It's like a long slide. That explains why I didn't get too hurt, she thought.

She pointed the light farther down the shaft. She saw nothing but more blackness. Belle shivered. She bit down on her lip to stop herself from bursting into tears.

"I'm going for help!" Ta'al called down. "Can you sit tight and wait for me?"

"Where else am I going to go?" Belle replied. Truthfully, she was afraid to be left here alone. But Ta'al had to leave, or she'd never get out of here.

Belle heard the crunching of pebbles beneath Ta'al's feet. And then there was silence. It was the heaviest silence she'd ever experienced. She pulled her knees to her chest and tried to breathe normally. She thought about her farm and her dad working on the posts with Melody.

She imagined Raider running around them barking in excitement. She thought about her mom, giving little Thea a bath in the kitchen sink. She pictured the sun sliding behind the rain clouds and the soothing coolness of the rain on her skin. She had to think of these things so that she wouldn't begin to cry or scream out in fear. But the tears came anyway, even though she didn't want them to.

She'd never felt so lonely in her life.

● ● ● ●

Belle had no idea how much time had passed. As she waited for Ta'al to return, her legs began to cramp up. She shined her light around and decided to stand up and stretch her legs.

"Okay, Belle," she said aloud to herself. Her voice echoed off the walls. It felt good to hear a sound. "If I have to wait around, I might as well explore a little."

With Ta'al's device in hand, she lit a path farther inside the shaft. She kept one hand above her on the ceiling in case the shaft grew smaller. She didn't want to bump her head. But to her surprise, after a few steps the ceiling seemed to disappear altogether. Belle shined her narrow beam of light high above her head.

"This is a cave," she said aloud. "Hellooo!"

She knew no one would answer. She wanted to hear the echo. And she was rewarded with several of them.

Hellooo, hellooo, helloooo . . . went the echo. It made her smile, just a little.

Belle pointed her light to the ground at her feet. She took a step, then another. Everything beneath her feet was black and gray. But suddenly, a glint of something silver caught her eye. She bent down to touch it. It was smooth and cold. It was also partially buried. She knelt down and brushed away as much dirt as she could, all the while shining her light on the silver object. Before long she noticed some kind of marking on it.

"That's an N," she said. There was writing on this object. The letter was large. She began to dig with her fingers. "And that's an A."

Belle looked around, found a flat stone, and used it to finish digging out the object. The more she dug, the bigger the object seemed to get.

What are you? she thought. She reached down and swept dirt off the object.

The letters were printed over a circle of stars. There was a red slash behind the letter *A*. There was also a white slash running between the *N* and *A*. Belle kept scraping at the symbol. The next letter looked like an *S*, but the rest of

it was buried too deep. She sat back, panting from her work. "N - A - S," she said. "I wonder if that's NASA, the old Earth space agency?" She'd read about that at her previous school on Earth. Space science had been her favorite subject there. She wished they could learn more about it here on Mars. But all they seemed to teach at school was agriculture and hybrid biology.

She got back on her feet and dusted herself off. This was probably a relic of history — left here when the first astronauts landed on Mars. Her heart skipped a beat. This was quite a discovery. She wondered if there was more to find down here.

Forgetting some of her fear, she moved farther into the darkness. She shuffled her feet through the pebbles and dust, just in case the ground gave way again. She began to think she had to be in a cave — a giant cave.

Then she heard something like the sound of trickling water, but it was so far away.

She swept her light around her. A hissing noise stopped her in her tracks. Belle thought for a moment that it might be steam gushing out from the under the ground, like the geysers she'd read about on Earth. But she didn't see any evidence of that. It was completely dry in the cave. The hissing grew louder, as if something was coming toward her. It wasn't steam. It sounded like a living thing — or several living things.

Belle screamed.

The sound of many feet scurrying and scuttling over the pebbles made her scream again. She turned back and ran. She hoped she was going the same direction she'd come from. It was so dark, she didn't know which way was which. Her foot caught on something, causing her to trip and fall on the hard ground.

"Who's out there?" she gasped.

She moved her light slowly in a wide arc while shuffling herself backward. She focused on slowing her breathing, so she could concentrate on whatever was in here with her.

The beam of light flowed over large rocks, cube-shaped stones, and tiny pebbles. Then, just for a second, she saw something. It looked like a spiky tail!

She shrieked.

The tail vanished into a pile of cube-shaped stones.

CHAPTER FOUR

:A MAJOR FIND:

The scuttling sound had stopped. But Belle kept her light fixed on the spot where the tail had disappeared. She was in no mood to encounter a new creature. It had been hard enough getting used to all of the strange farm animals on Mars. First it was giant horsels and ugly turkats. There were also the wiggling mealworms used as food for people

43

and animals, which made her squirm. And then Lucas had shown her how to find bugs that turkens liked to eat. She'd been creeped out by them ever since.

She definitely didn't want to meet another mystery creature. Especially not in this dark, spooky cave.

"Ta'al!" She tried shouting again. She did that once every few minutes, each time hoping that someone would shout back. But so far . . . nothing. Her voice was becoming hoarse, and all her tears had dried up. She took a deep breath and screamed as loudly as she could, not out of fear, but from frustration. She'd had enough of this cave.

"Belle!" She heard her friend's voice. It was faint, but it was definitely Ta'al.

"I'm here! Help me!" she shouted back.

"Hold on," Ta'al yelled. "Melody is here. She was looking for us in town. She sent a message to your Dad. He's on his way here."

"I am sending a mini-drone down to you," came the familiar voice of Belle's android. Melody's flat voice sent a calmness through Belle. She badly needed her friend's steady confidence. It was as comforting as hot cocoa on a cold winter's evening. Everything was going to be fine.

Within minutes, the welcome hum of a mini-drone greeted her. It flooded her area with more light than Ta'al's device could provide. Belle saw that she was indeed sitting before the mouth of a giant cave. And she could more clearly see the mysterious NASA object jutting out of the ground in front of her. It looked like part of a machine, or perhaps a land vehicle. Could it be an ancient rover?

The drone flew around the area where Belle sat, giving those above ground the information needed to rescue her. Melody's voice came through the drone's speaker. "Are you injured?"

"No, I'm okay. My raingear protected me," Belle replied.

"Are you able to climb up?" Melody asked.

"It's too steep," she said, moving back toward the spot where she had fallen. "And it's not straight up. There must be a bend in the shaft."

"You are correct," Melody said. "You fell quite a distance."

"Can you do something? I don't like it down here alone," Belle pleaded.

"I will attempt to come down to you," Melody said.

Belle held her breath as she waited. If her android were down here with her, things wouldn't be so bad.

A trickle of pebbles soon began rolling down the shaft. A few of them bounced off of Belle's shoes. Then a terrible rumbling sound filled the air. It sounded just like the moment when the ground swallowed her.

"No, stop!" she yelled.

But it was too late. A mass of rocks and dirt came tumbling down the shaft. Belle backed toward the cave entrance, tripped over a rock, and fell flat on her back. The rumbling went on for several seconds and then stopped. Silence filled the air again, along with dust, causing Belle to cough hard.

She sat up. The drone was shining its light toward the shaft she'd come through. But the shaft was gone. In its place was a wall of fallen rock and dirt.

She was trapped!

"Melody, where are you? Are you all right?" Belle cried. She wiped her face with the back of her hand and her mouth filled with dust. She spat it out onto the ground.

A few moments later the drone rotated to face her. It lowered its light beam.

"The shaft was more unstable than I thought," the android replied through the drone's speaker. "I caused it to collapse. I was almost buried, but managed to get out."

"What do we do now?" Belle could feel the walls of the cave start to close in on her. She knew it was only her fear that made her feel this way, but it felt too real.

"Don't panic," Ta'al said through the drone. She knew Belle all too well. "Your Dad is bringing help."

"I suggest, in the meantime, that we look for another entrance." Melody was full of good ideas.

"Yes!" Belle got to her feet. "There's a big cave down here. There should be more than one entrance." *Right?* She wasn't sure, but she had to be positive, or else she might just curl up and cry.

The drone and its wide beam of light brought her some relief. She also had Ta'al and Melody's voices to keep her company. She pointed out the NASA object to them.

"This must have been a landing site for the old Earth explorations," Ta'al said, trying to sound cheerful. "That's quite a valuable find."

Belle moved in farther, back to where she'd heard the hissing sounds earlier.

"There's something else down here," Belle said, recalling the tail. She also remembered that loud noises sent them scattering. She stomped her feet with each step. "Melody, are there any native life forms to Mars? Ones that hiss and have long tails?"

"None that I have seen in the databanks," Melody replied.

Belle stepped noisily through the chamber. There was no hissing, and no tails. Then she stopped. The drone's light lit up a lot of stones in front of her. The enormous cube-shaped stones were wider than she was tall. She ran her hand along the smooth surface of one stone. Some stones had cracks in them, forming hand-sized gaps. Belle avoided those, in case there were creatures hiding inside.

The stones could have been created by volcanic lava flows that cooled quickly. She'd learned about that back on Earth. But they could have also been made by humans or aliens. With the NASA objects she'd found earlier, it seemed logical that someone had crafted these stones. The drone swept its light beam around the area. There were dozens, if not hundreds of these same stones, all roughly the same size. Some were piled on top of each other to form columns. They certainly looked hand-made.

Belle faced the drone and shared her thoughts about the stones with her friends. "Either of those theories could be valid," Melody replied. "Is the cave filled with them?"

"It looks that way from here," Belle said.

She walked farther into the cave. The drone's light lit up a large area of the cave floor. Belle gasped.

Before her wasn't just a cave, but what looked like the ruins of an entire building, or even a city street. The drone flew high over it, lighting up a wide pathway.

"This place must have been lived in by people a long time ago," Belle said. "Amazing!"

"This is a remarkable find," Melody said.

"From what I can see, this looks like an old courtyard."
Ta'al's voice was filled with excitement. "And you said there
were creatures in the stones that hissed?"

"Yes, but I don't see them anymore," Belle replied.
"I hope they're too scared of me to come out again."

Belle craned her neck to see all around her. She was
standing in the middle of a large square. It certainly could
have been a courtyard from a long time ago. Cubical stones
were stacked up high in several places on both sides of her.
A couple of stones were cylindrical and jagged at the top,
like broken columns. She signaled at the drone to follow
her hand to light the ceiling and walls. There were carvings
with odd symbols everywhere.

As the drone hummed along and recorded what Belle
saw, she heard Ta'al exclaim.

"Belle, don't touch anything!" she cried.

"Why?" Belle asked, freezing in place.

"I think you've stumbled upon a Nabian holy site."

Belle's eyes widened. She stared at the symbols on the
walls. They did look a little like the Nabian writing she'd
seen in Ta'al's house.

"Belle, those hissing creatures?" Ta'al's voice quivered
with excitement, even through the drone's microphone.
"They must be guardians!"

"What are guardians?"

"They're legendary creatures," Ta'al said. "I never really believed them to be real."

"Oh, they're real, all right," Belle replied. "I saw a tail and heard them running around. Not to mention the hissing."

"That's incredible!" Ta'al exclaimed excitedly. "Nabians believe the guardians were tasked with protecting sacred relics. Belle, you could be standing right by some of the most holy items of the Nabian culture!"

The drone's light beam panned slowly around the cave. Belle twirled, following its movement. Everything made sense to her now. This was some kind of ancient site, buried underground. The stones might have formed as volcanic rocks, but they had been stacked to be used as columns or parts of buildings.

"I thought Nabians didn't come to Mars until after humans and Sulux came here," she said, looking up at the high ceiling. She hadn't noticed earlier, but there were symbols carved into every part of it. How could ancient Nabians carve symbols so high up? Could they fly?

"That's what I thought too," Ta'al said. "You don't think this was one of the reasons my people fought the Sulux, do you?"

Hissss! Hisssss!

Belle froze. The sound was coming from behind her. It grew louder with each breath.

"Ta'al?" she whispered to the drone. "The guardians don't . . . *eat people*, do they?"

Belle turned around very slowly. The light from the drone dimmed, but only so that it wasn't too glaring. *Was Ta'al doing that on purpose to avoid scaring the creatures?*

As Belle turned, she saw something gleaming in the dark. A pair of round eyes reflected the light from the drone. They were golden-colored, with dark, vertical slits in the middle. All the breath in Belle's lungs seemed to evaporate. Those gold eyes belonged to the biggest, scariest lizard she'd ever seen!

CHAPTER FIVE
:A HISTORIC SITE:

"Don't move!" Ta'al's voice came through the drone's speaker. "They only attack if they think you're going to hurt them."

"Um, okay. But what if I think they're going to hurt me?" Belle did her best to imitate a statue. "Did you know they have really sharp claws?"

She stared at the lizard. As with everything else on Mursu, this creature was huge, about the size of Raider.

but with shorter legs. It had sharp-looking ridges running down its back, and its forked tongue flicked at her every few seconds. Its front feet had five long toes tipped with wicked-looking claws. The lizard stretched out one foot with its claws spread out wide, as if it was getting ready to grab her.

The drone lowered to Belle's waist level and placed itself between her and the lizard. Ta'al's voice came through the drone. It sounded like she was singing something in her own language. It was very soothing. The lizard cocked its head to one side. It seemed to be listening to Ta'al's song. For a second, the creature looked quite harmless to Belle.

Suddenly the lizard took a step toward Belle. She took a step back. Some pebbles came loose beneath her feet and rippled down toward the lizard. The pebbles startled the reptile, and it lunged at Belle.

She screamed. The drone turned to face Belle.

"Are you all right?" Melody's voice came through the drone's speaker.

Belle couldn't answer. She was too busy scurrying away from the oncoming creature. The lizard hissed loudly and scuttled up to her feet. The drone rotated to focus on the lizard. Every spike along its back was lit up

by the drone's light. The creature flicked its tail around its body, scattering pebbles in all directions. Its tongue shot out and brushed Belle's leg. She screamed again, this time louder and longer. The lizard spun away from her, whipping its tail against both of Belle's legs. The spikes pierced through her trousers and scratched her skin. Belle was so scared, she froze. She couldn't scream anymore, and she had nowhere to run. All she could do was shut her eyes and prepare for the worst.

She breathed in . . . and out. In . . . and out.

Nothing happened.

She opened one eye and peeked down at her feet. The lizard stood several feet away and watched her with its head tilted to the side. After a few seconds, it casually turned and ambled away from her, disappearing into the darkness.

"Follow it!" Ta'al called through the drone. "It knows the way out!"

"What?" Belle couldn't believe her ears. She had barely escaped being eaten alive, and now she was supposed to follow the scary creature?

"Go!" Melody agreed with Ta'al.

Belle shoved all her fear aside and ran after the lizard. Its heavy tail swished side to side, creating a visible path through the dusty ground for Belle to follow. Even with the

drone to light her way, the path grew darker ahead. Belle
was seriously doubting Ta'al's advice, but then she saw a
tiny glimmer of light ahead.

Suddenly more hissing sounds filled the cave. Belle
stopped walking.

"Keep going," Ta'al said. "They'll leave you alone now."

Belle heard Ta'al add, "I hope," quietly to Melody. That
didn't help.

But with each step, the light ahead seemed to glow
bigger and brighter.

"I see the entrance," Melody said through the drone.
"Follow that light, Belle." The drone flew ahead of her.

Belle took a deep breath and counted to three. She
hoped Ta'al was right. She ran hard toward the light.

When Belle burst through the cave entrance, she
gratefully inhaled the fresh air. The warmth of the Martian
sun had never felt so good on her face. Overcome with
relief, she laughed and cried at the same time. Behind her,
Melody came hovering over. Belle hugged her android
for a really long time. When Ta'al came running up, she
hugged her too.

"For a while I thought I was going to be trapped in
there forever!" Belle wiped her sticky face with the back of
her hand.

"Look at your face!" Ta'al laughed. "You're streaked with red clay."

Belle laughed too. And then began to cry again. Melody insisted that Belle sit and rest while she investigated the mouth of the cave. She walked around the hole in the hillside that Belle had just escaped from and took holo-images of everything.

"So, you believe this is a sacred Nabian site?" Belle asked Ta'al, when she got bored watching Melody.

"It could be," she said. "It would explain the guardian, and how the old lullaby worked to charm it."

Belle wanted to say that it could've all been a big, lucky coincidence. But she didn't want to risk insulting her best friend.

"I found evidence of human activity down there too," Belle said, explaining about the NASA object. "But that would mean that humans knew about the Nabian site long ago. If that's true, why do the records say that no living species existed on Mars before humans lived here?"

"That's a very good question," Ta'al said. "I think my parents would be interested in the answer."

"But that was more than two hundred years ago. Do you think it still matters?" Belle asked.

Ta'al patted Belle's knee. "History always matters," she said. Then she stood up and went to examine the mouth of the cave. Belle lay back down and closed her eyes. She had never been so happy to soak in the sunshine.

A little while later Yun arrived. He brought Paddy and Myra Walker, Lucas' parents, with him. They had Loki and a ton of rope with them. When they saw Belle resting on the boulder, safe and above ground, they clapped and sighed in relief.

"You are one lucky girl," Paddy Walker exclaimed, as he eyed the small cave mouth that Belle had crawled out of.

"I want to know every detail of your adventure," Yun said, holding his daughter. "Your mother is worried sick. She couldn't leave Thea at home alone, but she very much wanted to come too."

"I'm fine," Belle said. "Thanks to Ta'al and Melody."

Yun insisted that Belle and Ta'al ride Loki all the way home. It was bumpy because of his unusual gait, but Belle was too tired to care.

When they reached the house, Zara had baked a huge batch of Belle's favorite muffins. Belle and Ta'al munched on the muffins as they told their tale. The adults listened closely to every detail.

"Lucas will be sorry he missed this story," Paddy said. "I'll be sure to send him over tomorrow morning so you can retell it."

Myra Walker had been very quiet the whole time. She'd listened very carefully to everything that Belle and Ta'al had described. Just as the Walkers stood up to leave, she turned to Belle.

"I think you have made a very important discovery." She touched Belle's face, staring at her with her large lilac eyes. "We should inform the authorities. I believe they would be interested in excavating this site."

"But if it is a Nabian holy site, we will need our high council to be involved," Ta'al said.

Myra smiled at her, but it was a strange smile. Belle wasn't sure what was going on. Still, she didn't want to be rude to Myra. She really liked Lucas' mom.

That night, before the girls fell asleep in Belle's room, Belle asked Ta'al if she'd talked to her parents about their find.

"I did," she said. "And I sent all our video footage to them." She lay in her bed staring at the ceiling of Belle's room, unblinking.

"And?" Belle didn't want to push Ta'al to talk, but her curiosity was too much to contain. If this site was part of the reason for the feud between the Sulux and the Nabians, excavating it might cause arguments as well.

Ta'al rolled over onto her side to face Belle. She had a very serious look in her eyes.

"My parents have cut short their tour of Lunar Colony," she said. "And they're on their way home as we speak."

Sol 92/Summer, Mars Cycle 106

It turns out my adventure underground only lasted two and a half hours. It felt more like two and a half sols! Every time I shut my eyes, I see those guardian lizards . . . hundreds of them. And they're all chasing me. I can still feel the flick of its tongue on my leg and its sharp tail ridges.

But now that I think about it, I wonder if it actually helped me to get out? I wonder if Ta'al actually communicated with it and asked for its help? In which case, it's not a bad animal. It saved me.

Who knows?

All I know is that I stumbled upon something important. I can't wait to see what happens next.

CHAPTER SIX
:WHOSE RELICS?:

Myra Walker had been correct. The authorities were very interested in Belle's discovery. Two days later, not only had Taral's parents returned, but three huge Protector androids also showed up at the Songs' doorstep. Along with them came a representative of the Olympus regional government and a Saline council member. Their arrival was so unusual that several neighbors came by to see what was going on as well.

There wasn't enough space in the Song house to seat everyone. And everyone insisted on talking at the same time. It was a good thing Thea had her Nabian crib shield. She slept through the entire meeting.

A tall Martian woman raised her hand. The Protectors came to attention and stomped their robot legs loudly. It scared everyone into silence.

"I am Secretary Sukanya, aide to the governor of Olympia," the woman said. "I appreciate everyone's interest in this historic discovery, but Representative Valere and I would like to interview the child who found the relics."

She paused to look everyone in the eye.

"In private," she added.

Belle did not appreciate being referred to as "the child". She was more than thirteen years old, after all.

The Protectors ushered the neighbors out of the Song house. The Walkers didn't look happy to leave. Belle whispered to Lucas that she'd fill him in on everything as soon as she could.

"Meet me by the large apple tree at the end of our farm in an hour," she said.

Lucas winked at her as he left with his parents.

The only other people allowed to remain were Ta'al's parents — So'ark, He'ern, and Fa'erz. They were the only people in the room who were almost as tall as the Protectors. They towered over the government officials, and looked intimidating in their long, flowing robes.

Everybody listened intently as Belle told her story once more. Ta'al and Melody added details where necessary.

"Can you show us the site?" Secretary Sukanya asked. The red rings around her irises glowed under the dim house lights.

"Of course," Belle said. Ta'al had mapped out the location of the site as they rode home on Loki's back.

"Then we must go immediately," Representative Valere said. He was Sulux, with the same copper-colored hair as Myra Walker. He had very distinct ridges on his head and arms. It made him look as if he had natural armor.

So'ark, Ta'al's mother, stepped forward. "There is the matter of jurisdiction." She sounded very serious. "If this is a Nabian site, then it should be our representative that investigates. Sulux will have no place inside."

Secretary Sukanya exhaled loudly. "This is not the place for this argument. Mars is a human colony, and as the governor's representative, I have jurisdiction here."

"If what the child says is accurate," He'ern added, "the relics are located outside of the terraformed area. That makes it *para-ta-num-peia* — no man's land."

Belle cringed at the word "child" again. But she knew it was better to keep silent.

"And access to a sacred Nabian site is not included in the Martian-Sulux Agreement," Fa'erz said.

"Of course it isn't included," Valere said. "That's because no one knew there might be a Nabian site on Mars."

"We don't even know for sure that it *is* Nabian," Sukanya added.

So'ark rose to her full height. Everyone looked up at her. "This is a very troubling argument. According to my daughter, and the holo-vid evidence, it is most likely a holy Nabian site. So, I must insist, quite firmly, that you wait for the Nabian representative before you enter the cave. I am deeply concerned that without our council's involvement, the site may be desecrated."

All three of Ta'al's parents stood together, and said, "We cannot allow it."

There was a long silence following the Nabians' stand. Belle was surprised at their reaction. She had never seen Ta'al's family so determined before.

Finally, it was Yun that broke the silence and tension. "Well, how about something to drink? All this talk is thirsty work," he said with a smile. "Besides, I'm pretty sure nobody wants a serious argument this early in the day."

Belle's dad liked to use humor to ease tense moments. She thought it was amusing, even though she sometimes didn't understand half of what he said. But she wasn't sure it worked this time.

"Yes, why don't we discuss it over tea?" Zara suggested, as Melody entered with a tray of tea and snacks. This was Belle's mom's way of solving problems. It seemed to work better than her dad's attempt at humor.

The two officials appeared relieved by the distraction. Ta'al's family calmly sat down. The tension in the room relaxed and soon they were chatting politely. Meanwhile, the Protectors stood by the wall with their red eyes constantly scanning the room.

About half an hour into the conversation, Belle was growing bored. When Yun put up a holo-map of the region in front of the guests, Belle knew this was her chance.

"I need to feed Raider and Loki," she said to her parents. "Can Ta'al come and help me?"

Nobody seemed to mind if the girls left for a while, as long as Melody accompanied them.

"I couldn't stand listening to them talk anymore," Belle said as they headed for the stable.

"I thought it was interesting," Ta'al said. "It's important to us as Nabians what happens to these relics."

"I found it very interesting as well," Melody added.

"If they *are* Nabian," Belle said.

"Of course they are." Ta'al sounded surprised at Belle's doubt. "I recognized them." She looked to Melody to confirm it.

Melody's eyes turned green as she scanned her inner databanks. "I am unable to find any claims of Nabians living on Mars prior to human colonization. But the carvings did have a strong resemblance to Nabian script."

Belle pulled open the stable door and Raider jumped out at her. He ran around the yard barking happily.

"There are definitely human relics in the cave too," Belle said. "We should have the right to study them as well."

"The Nabian relics are far more ancient and would have been there long before the human ones," Ta'al responded. "For all we know, the humans invaded our site. They may have removed some items too."

"Well, I think the representatives should be allowed to look at everything before making a decision." Belle was getting tired of this argument.

Ta'al didn't reply. Belle could tell she was annoyed.

"Look at us," Belle said, smiling. She wanted to patch things up with her friend. "Let's not fight. Let's leave the decisions to the grown-ups."

"That is the best idea," Melody agreed.

Ta'al smoothed out her robe, and still said nothing. Belle thought it best to leave her alone and went about feeding the animals. She moved on to the big barn to check on the turken fowl that she was raising for her science project with Lucas.

"Oh!" she exclaimed suddenly. "I completely forgot about Lucas!"

The girls ran to the end of the Song farm to a cluster of tall, thick-trunked trees. Melody ambled along slowly. Ta'al lagged behind, and Belle reached the trees first. Lucas was sitting up in the apple tree, munching on a giant fruit.

"It took you long enough to get here," he complained. "I've been waiting for you to show me this cave you found."

Belle looked back toward Ta'al as she ran up to them. She knew Ta'al wouldn't be happy with Lucas' idea.

"Come on, Belle, let's go" Lucas said. He took her hand and playfully tugged her in the direction of the site. As he did so, Belle's heart skipped a beat and her face heated up. She kicked the pebbles at her feet.

"I guess I could show you where I fell," she said, looking toward Ta'al. "That should be okay, right?"

Ta'al shrugged. Melody began to protest, but Belle pleaded with her until she agreed to let them go.

"All right!" Lucas was excited. "You're the best, Belle!"
Belle grinned.

"I will send a message to inform your parents,"
Melody said. Her eyes began to turn blue, which was her
communication mode.

"Please wait, Melody," Belle said. "The representatives
won't like it, and I don't want to get my parents in trouble."

Melody accepted that argument. "I will give you a
thirty-minute head start. But I must message them before
we lose communications out there."

Lucas ran ahead. "The Senns want to come too. I'll just
go get them."

What? Belle felt the heat again, but this time it came
from a fire in her stomach. Ta'al pressed her palms to her
temples and glared at the ground.

"You'd better not let them inside," she warned Belle.

"I *won't!*" Belle was shocked at hearing the anger in her
own voice. She had never yelled at Ta'al before. But then,
she'd also never seen Ta'al so angry before either.

CHAPTER SEVEN

::NEW DISCOVERIES::

Lucas, Ava, and the twins met Ta'al, Belle, and
Melody just outside the school building. Belle led the
way to the site. Ta'al lagged behind everyone else, asking
Melody questions along the way.

"How far are we going?" Ava complained every ten
minutes. Belle wanted to tell her to go home if she wasn't
interested in coming along. But she bit her tongue and
tried hard to remember her manners.

The twins shoved each other a lot and told silly jokes all the way to the site. They made everyone laugh, and the journey didn't feel so long. When they finally arrived at the hole that Belle had fallen through, she felt dizzy. Looking down into the darkness, she couldn't believe it had actually happened. It felt as if the entire experience had been a bad dream.

"So, there are these enormous lizards in there," Belle said, trying to distract herself from the dizziness.

"Cool!" the boys exclaimed. They took turns sticking their heads in the gap.

"Eew!" Ava scrunched up her nose. She clung onto Belle's arm. "You were so brave to survive down there, all by yourself."

Belle didn't know what to say. All of a sudden Ava was acting like they were best friends. Belle looked for Ta'al to see what she was thinking. But Ta'al was sitting on a rock in the distance, talking to Melody about something. She didn't even look up at Belle.

"Tell me every detail about what happened to you down there," Ava said. "You are officially my hero. Or heroine. Whatever."

Belle repeated her story once again. Even the twins quieted down and listened with mouths open.

"You have to take us inside the cave," Aiden said when Belle finished her tale.

"Oh yes!" Ava clapped her hands. She grabbed Belle's hand with both of hers. "Please! You must."

Alex and Lucas joined in with the begging. Belle looked over at Ta'al. Her best friend's eyes, which usually reflected her surroundings, were dark and cloudy. She was angry. Not just upset, but seriously fuming. Belle knew she had to refuse the others.

"Is this it?" Belle heard Lucas' voice calling from a distance. While she had been gathering up the courage to say no to Ava and her brothers, Lucas had run off and found the cave entrance. He was jumping up and down and pointing at the place where Belle had escaped the cave.

"Wait!" Belle ran up to him. The others followed. "We can't go in. We have to wait for the officials first."

"Oh, come on," Lucas said, with a mischievous grin. "We won't touch anything, and we won't tell."

"Absolutely," Ava said. She put her hands together, as if begging for Belle's permission. "You had such an amazing adventure. You'd want to share that with your good friends, wouldn't you?"

"Yeah!" pleaded the twins. "You have to show us how you braved the cave!"

Belle could feel her face heat up. She wasn't used to getting so much attention. She kind of enjoyed it. She twisted back and forth, looking over at Ta'al and Melody, and then at the others. Ta'al wouldn't look at her. Belle was frustrated. All Ta'al seemed to care about was who owned the relics.

"All right," Belle said at last. "But we can only look. Don't touch anything."

Everyone cheered. Everyone except Ta'al.

Lucas and the twins helped pull away some of the rocks around the cave entrance to make room to crawl through. When Belle had climbed out before, she hadn't realized that the gap was so narrow. She was a little surprised that she had squeezed through it. But at the time she had been desperate to get out.

Now she was eager to get back in. Well, kind of eager. She was still afraid of the lizard creatures, and she felt guilty about making Ta'al angry. But she thought she should at least try to act brave enough to show her new friends her discovery.

"Don't forget," she said, as they climbed inside one at a time, "absolutely no touching anything."

Alex and Aiden went first, switching on their wrist lamps. Lucas followed. Ava had brought a headlamp, which she strapped to her forehead. Melody had her own lighting, which had the widest beam. Belle hung on to her android, since she was the only one without her own light.

The last person to enter the cave was Ta'al. Her large eyes allowed her to see well enough in the dim light.

"I only saw it through the drone's camera," she said, without looking at Belle. "I want to see it with my own eyes. The representatives may not let me in later."

Belle smiled secretly to herself. Maybe Ta'al wouldn't be too mad at her anymore.

"Wow!" Lucas exclaimed as he aimed his own headlamp at the large cavern in front of them. "Look at those columns. It looks like a giant's house."

Ta'al climbed over a couple of boulders to look at the wall carvings. She ran her hand over some of the symbols.

"I can almost read these," she said. "They're an ancient form of our language. I'm certain now that this is a Nabian site."

She turned to examine the column that Melody and Belle were looking at.

"See this design?" Ta'al said. "We have this same symbol in our home."

Belle nodded. It did look familiar.

Lucas came over to their side. "Huh, that's weird. We have this design in our home too," he said. "I wonder if this could actually be a Sulux site?"

"No!" Ta'al's voice echoed off the cave walls. It made Belle jump. Lucas took a step back.

"Why are you mad at me?" he said. "I'm just telling you what I know."

Ta'al made a scowling face and walked farther into the cave by herself.

"I've never seen her so upset," Belle whispered quietly to Melody.

"Nabians are very serious about their cultural sites," Melody replied. "They lost a lot in the wars."

"Wars?" Belle was shocked. "I thought Nabians were a peaceful race."

"They are," Melody said. "But even peaceful races get drawn into wars when their home worlds are at stake. The Nabian home world is all but destroyed."

Belle noted to herself that she should find out more when they got home. She wanted to know more about the Nabian planet.

Ava appeared at Belle's side. She wrapped her arm around Belle's shoulders.

"You have to show me these lizards," she said. "I'm scared of them, but I'll hide behind you." She made a silly giggling sound. It grated on Belle's nerves. But she didn't show it. She was curious about Ava's sudden friendliness.

Belle led the group farther into the cave, to the point where she last saw the lizard that led her out. She put her finger to her lips.

"Stay very still," she whispered. "They don't like loud noises. It scares them."

They kept as quiet and still as possible for a long minute. Melody dimmed her light too. Nothing happened. Ava started to giggle again. She gripped Belle's arm and spoke directly into her ear.

"I don't see anything," Ava whispered.

"Shh!" Belle put her finger to her lip again.

"For how long?" Ava asked.

"I don't know," Belle said.

"Bet they aren't even real," one of the twins said.

"I think you made them up to make things more interesting," the other one said.

Belle couldn't believe her ears. They were being so rude!

"Nah!" Lucas jumped in. "Belle doesn't make stuff up like that. If she said she saw them, then I believe her."

Belle smiled at Lucas. It seemed silly now that she hadn't liked him much when they first met.

"Look over here!" Ta'al's voice echoed through the cave. She was standing over something.

Belle and the others went to her side. Half buried in the dirt was what looked like a set of wheels. They seemed ancient, and Belle could tell they were definitely from Earth. She had seen hologram images of vehicles with these kinds of wheels.

"And over here," Ta'al said. She sounded excited. It made Belle feel better. At least her friend wasn't angry anymore. "Tracks. They go around the perimeter of the cave. They must have been undisturbed for years. They're perfectly imprinted in the ground."

Belle and Lucas walked alongside the tracks. They made an interesting pattern on the ground — a series of dashes and dots.

"This resembles an old Earth code," Melody said, moving next to them.

"Yes!" Belle recognized it. "It's Morse code!" She'd gone through a phase in the fourth grade when she was crazy about spy stories. She'd studied all kinds of codes and encryptions.

She looked closer at the tread marks. After a minute she could make out a pattern. If she remembered the code correctly, it looked like the pattern spelled out N-A-S-A, just like the object she found near the shaft.

"This was definitely made by a human vehicle," she said.

"Do you realize what this means?" Ta'al's eyes were wide as she stared at the tracks. "It means that humans knew about the Nabian site before they colonized Mars. They knew someone else had been here before them."

"So?" Belle wasn't sure where Ta'al was going with this.

"It means they kept it a secret!" Ta'al was clearly angry again. "They told everyone that there was no life on Mars so they could claim it for themselves. Mars should never have belonged to humans."

"What's that supposed to mean?" Lucas asked.

"Yeah, so what? Do you think humans should just leave Mars and go back to Earth or something?" Alex added.

"I didn't say that," Ta'al responded angrily. "But Nabians were here first. We should have had a chance to build our own colony here."

Belle didn't understand what point her friend was trying to make. Before Mars was terraformed, nothing could live there. Nobody else wanted it, so it became an Earth colony.

At the time, the Sulux and Nabians were just visitors to Mars. Why was Ta'al so angry?

Ta'al's words didn't just irritate Belle. The Senns and Lucas were also pretty mad. They started to argue with Ta'al. All kinds of opinions were batted back and forth. Belle couldn't stand it. She grabbed Melody and went off to explore on her own.

She trudged past the large columns and walked into a section of the cave she hadn't seen before. There was a large column that was still intact. It was shaped differently than the others. Belle wondered if it was special somehow. She walked around it, running her hand over the grooves. On the far side of the column was a carving of two large faces in the stone. Belle stared at the carving. She had Melody shine her light on it so she could study it more closely.

The faces were familiar. One had two big eyes and a large, dark mouth. Its nostrils were on its forehead, just like Ta'al and her family. It was definitely Nabian. The other face was clearly Sulux. The two faces were close, almost touching. And they were smiling as if they liked each other.

"Hey, everyone, come over here!" she called. She had to shout at the others two more times before they stopped arguing. "You need to see this!"

When the others made their way over to Belle, Ta'al gaped at the sculpture of the faces.

"Doesn't this show that Nabians and Sulux were friends at one time?" Belle asked.

"Let's look for more of these," Lucas suggested. "It's definitely not what I've been taught."

They spread out and began searching for more carvings of Nabian and Sulux figures. Even Ava became absorbed in their mission. Within minutes, everyone had found something. Carvings in the walls, the ceilings, and the floors showed pictures of Nabians and Sulux working and living together. Ta'al even found a full sculpture of what looked like a family.

"I don't believe this," she gasped. "Two parents are Nabian, but the third is Sulux! I've never heard of such a thing."

They stared in silence at their findings.

"So Nabians and Sulux were once friends," Belle said. "What happened to change that?"

Lucas looked at Ta'al, who looked back at him. They both shrugged.

"Ta'al and I became friends," Lucas said. "Maybe we weren't the first."

Ta'al sighed and let a smile sneak onto her lips.

"I will take holo-vid recordings of everything," Melody said.

"Hello! Is there anyone in there?" Somebody was calling from outside the cave.

The adults had arrived. Belle swallowed. She knew she would be in awful trouble. Even Ta'al and Lucas looked nervous. The Senns didn't seem to notice.

"We should go back outside," Belle said, fearing what she might have to face there.

They walked carefully around the carvings and tread marks on the ground. Before they reached the mouth of the cave, one of the twins called out in excitement.

"Hey, Alex. Look what I caught!" he cried.

They shined their lights at Aiden. His hands were cupped together and he was grinning mischievously.

"No way!" Alex said, going to his brother's side. "Where did you find it? I want one!"

Belle stepped a little closer. In Aiden's hands was a baby lizard. It hissed loudly and flicked its tongue nervously at the air.

"Put that down, *now!*" Ta'al yelled. "Its mother will come after you!"

Suddenly the cave was filled with loud hissing. The sound echoed off the walls and filled their ears.

Ava screamed. Melody flashed her light everywhere, but they couldn't see any lizards.

The hissing just grew louder.

"She's right, Aiden. You should put that baby lizard down," Lucas suggested.

"We should get out of here," Belle said.

But instead of putting the baby down, Aiden took a step toward the cave entrance. As soon as he did, the adult lizards appeared. Hundreds of lizard eyes stared at them from every crack in every stone. Tongues flicked, making a crackling sound that sent chills through Belle.

"Run!" Ta'al cried.

Everyone bolted as fast as they could toward the entrance. The lizards followed. Their tails swished against the floor, adding to the sound of their hissing. Then Belle felt the ground trembling under her feet, as if an earthquake was coming.

She turned to look. All the lizard feet shuffling after the kids were causing the floor to vibrate.

"Put that baby down!" Belle yelled one more time. "Or they'll eat us!"

All the others started to yell at Aiden too. As he reached the cave mouth, he turned around and saw the

lizards getting closer. In a few seconds, the kids would be surrounded by every creature in the cave.

Aiden yelped and dropped the baby lizard. It fell to the rocky ground with a slap. Then it scuttled toward the adult lizards and disappeared into a crack in the rock. Instantly, the grown lizards scattered. As suddenly as they had appeared, every one of them vanished.

The cave was silent, except for the sound of the kids' heavy breathing.

"I can't believe we were almost eaten by giant lizards," Lucas said breathlessly.

One by one, each kid began to giggle as the fear of the lizards began to drain from them. They climbed out of the cave mouth. When they emerged into the dim evening light, they were all laughing.

However, Secretary Sukanya, Representative Valere, Ta'al's parents, and Yun were all standing outside with stern faces.

They did not look pleased — not one bit.

When the adults stopped yelling at us, we explained what we had found. Melody showed them her holo-vid footage. That shut them all up very quickly. Well, most of them anyway.

Dad was furious that I "put my friends in danger." He insisted that I head straight home with him. I tried to explain that Lucas, Ava, and her brothers had practically forced me to show them the cave. But would he listen? No!

When we parted, Ta'al whispered to me that she was disappointed that I had broken my promise not to disturb the site. I think she was just mad about the lizards. (Even worse, nobody believed us about that. They said the lizards were legendary animals and we'd made them up!)

Dad programmed Melody to keep me grounded in the house for the next two sols. Can you believe that? I can't even go above ground to feed Loki and the turkens! Well, two can play this game. I won't just be grounded in the house. I'm going to stay inside my room until I'm ungrounded. Dad won't see me at all. That'll show him!

Discovering the site and the relics has made everyone behave in such a weird way. I wish I'd never found it.

CHAPTER EIGHT
:THE COST:
OF FAME

Belle was serious about staying in her room. She absolutely refused to leave her bedroom for two whole days. She even ate in her room. She made Melody bring in trays and take away the empty ones. She refused to speak to her father, but that didn't stop him from coming into her room and lecturing her over and over again. He kept talking about the dangers of wandering off to the barren lands and putting herself and others at risk.

But by the third day, her resolve began to wear down. Boredom crept in, and she couldn't wait until it was a school day. At least then she wouldn't have to stay cooped up in her room like this.

Belle also desperately wanted to find out what was happening with the cave and the relics inside. And she wanted to know how Ta'al was doing, as well as what the shared Sulux and Nabian carvings in the cave meant. Her parents wouldn't tell her a thing. Even worse, Melody wouldn't say anything either.

Finally a school day arrived and Belle was allowed out of the house.

"Melody will walk you to school," Belle's mom told her. "And she'll meet you on the way back too."

"Mom!" Belle wailed. "I'm not a child anymore. I need some freedom."

Zara put her arm around Belle's shoulders. "I know you're growing up, Belle, but since moving to Mars, you've managed to get yourself into a lot of scrapes. We really just want you to be safe . . . and to obey the rules." She sighed. "It's not just for your safety. This time you put your friends in danger —"

"But they made me!" Belle cut in. She couldn't bear to hear the same lecture from her mom too.

Her mother quickly raised one finger. "Plus, you made a lot of people, very important people, very angry."

Belle had no reply for that. She'd never seen adults lose their cool the way the two government representatives had that day.

"We don't like keeping you in the house for so long. But how else can we get this message across to you? This is a dangerous planet." Zara shook her head. "I really hope you've learned your lesson this time."

Belle nodded. She felt she had learned her lesson. But she had a feeling this wouldn't be the last time she found herself in trouble. Her natural curiosity was just too strong. And trouble seemed to follow her around like Raider did.

Lucas wasn't there to meet her on the way to school. Neither was Ta'al.

"Perhaps they believed you were still confined to your room," Melody said.

It was a long, lonely walk. When she entered the school building, there were a lot of people outside Principal Yuko's office, including Yun. As soon as Belle's dad saw her, he waved her over. Her stomach made a somersault. Was she in trouble again already?

"Belle, there are some people here who would like to speak to you," Yun said. He introduced her to two human

Martians, a Sulux woman, and a third person from an alien race she hadn't seen before. This alien was a small, doll-like person.

Ms.Yuko introduced them, but Belle couldn't follow all their names. "They're journalists," she said, "and they would like to interview you about your discovery."

Ms. Yuko explained that everyone thought it was best to meet at the school, since there was more space there.

"And we don't want to upset your little sister," she added, then turned to the others. "You may use a spare classroom." Ms. Yuko spoke with a big grin. She enjoyed the attention that the school was getting.

Yun walked with Belle to room number four. As she passed room number one, she peeked through the open door. Her classmates were standing by the door. They waved as she passed by. Lucas was beaming. Ava looked like she was going to faint from the excitement.

"That's my best friend!" Ava yelled to the journalists.

Belle cringed. She looked for her real best friend. Ta'al stood at the back of the line of classmates. She looked very serious. Belle's heart dropped. Ta'al was still mad at her.

Yun sat by Belle through all the questions. One by one, the journalists came into the room and asked her every detail about her fall into the shaft and what she had seen inside the cave. Belle repeated her story for each journalist. She learned quickly to speak to their holo-cameras and not to look at the faces of the journalists. She sat up so straight that her back was aching by the third interview.

When there was a break between journalists three and four, she turned to her dad.

"Has anyone been back into the cave since we were there last?" she asked.

Yun nodded. He pulled out his datapad. "Secretary Sukanya agreed to wait for the Nabian representative to arrive before entering the cave. They did find human relics, but what was most interesting was this."

He flicked on his datapad, and showed her footage of the different officials exploring the cave. They stopped at the same carvings that Belle and her friends had seen. The expression on their faces was the same as that on Ta'al's. Disbelief and surprise.

"Your discovery made them realize that before their feuds and wars, the Nabians and Sulux were friends." Yun patted Belle on the head. Normally, she would hate that, but today she didn't mind. "And not just friends. It turns out that they may actually be related! They have a lot to talk about over the coming days and weeks . . . maybe even years."

"That's not surprising," Belle said, thinking about all she'd seen. "It makes sense, actually. Their home worlds are in the same solar system. Like Earth and Mars. They were bound to have some kind of connection."

Yun nodded again. "That's an impressive conclusion," he said. "You really are growing up, aren't you?"

"I've tried to tell you!" Belle rolled her eyes. Then she laughed and gave her dad a hug.

"The only ones who might get into trouble are the humans," Yun said as he waved in the last journalist. "They'll have to explain what they knew before colonization, but it was such a long time ago, we may never know."

The fourth journalist came into the room. Belle prepared to repeat her story for the last time — she hoped.

By the time Belle got back to class, Ms. Polley was finishing up the microbiology lecture. She was about to announce the results of the science fair projects. As Belle walked in, she was met with an unpleasant surprise. Ta'al wasn't sitting in her usual desk next to Belle's. Ava was! Brill was back in his seat next to Lucas, and Ta'al was sitting all alone. What had happened?

Belle tried to catch Ta'al's eye but she wouldn't look at her. Belle sighed. A heaviness filled her chest. She had so much to tell Ta'al, but her friend was still mad at her.

She didn't care anymore who won the science fair. She just wanted to talk to her friend.

Ava leaned over. "I asked Ms. Polley to let me sit here," she whispered. "I told her we were best friends, and I insisted on sitting next to you."

Belle couldn't even look at Ava. She had no idea why Ms. Polley would listen to her or why Ava thought they were best friends.

"The journalists will be coming to take pictures of you," Ava said. "Maybe you could ask them to take some photos with me too. Then everyone will know we're best friends."

Belle finally understood what Ava was up to. Ava only cared about being famous. But Belle didn't think fame was all it was made out to be. It was tiring.

Before long the four journalists stepped into the classroom.

"Just act normal," the Sulux journalist said. "Pretend we're not here."

Belle did her best to follow the journalist's advice. But Ava clearly didn't want to. She giggled and talked really loudly. She raised her hand, even when Ms. Polley hadn't asked a question. Even Lucas and the boys started acting like clowns to get the journalists' attention. Ta'al looked annoyed the entire time.

Sol 96/Summer, Mars Cycle 106

I don't know how, but Ta'al managed to avoid me the entire school day. She disappeared at lunchtime. I searched everywhere for her, but I couldn't find her. It didn't help that Ava was hanging around me the whole time. I almost wish she still had a crush on Lucas. But he told me she stopped liking him when he showed her his bug collection. Apparently, she's more scared of them than I was when I first moved here. He thought it was funny.

To make things worse, no one in our class won the science fair. It went to a high schooler who invented some kind of cloning machine. Ms. Polley said that the turken feed project that Lucas and I worked on received a "special mention" — whatever that means. And there was no mention at all of mine and Ta'al's Petripuff project. I guess they're not interested in defensive weapons.

After school, Ta'al ran ahead of me. I couldn't run and catch up to her, because Melody came to fetch me. She insisted I go straight home. Then I spent the rest of the day helping mom with Thea. I still have to help her, but she can almost sit up on her own!

CHAPTER NINE
:TRUE FRIENDS:

For the next few days, Belle's home felt like a tourist destination. Strange people dropped by to talk about the cave find. Scientists and archeologists from Tharsis City and Utopia kept stopping at the Songs' farm to share the discoveries they were making at the cave. Some of them even brought small artifacts with them. Yun and Zara were very interested, but Belle was sick of them. She missed her best friend. She would have traded all the artifacts on Mars for a chance to talk to Ta'al again.

One afternoon, Belle finally had enough of strangers visiting her house. Her parents must have pitied her, because they actually allowed her to go back to the ancient site to watch the work being done there. However, Melody was given strict orders not to allow Belle to go inside.

When they arrived at the cave site, Belle was amazed at the number of people there. Large crowds mingled around laser fences that had been put in place by the Protectors. The cave had been sealed off to the public, and only specialists and government officials were allowed in. Scientists went back and forth, some carrying large items. But they mostly carried small items in boxes. The scientists all wore facemasks and gloves. Belle asked Melody why they wore the special equipment.

"They do not want to contaminate any of the artifacts," Melody explained. "Once the pieces arrive at the museum, scientists will study them under controlled lab conditions."

"But wouldn't it be better to just leave them alone?" Belle remembered how Ta'al was upset at the thought of the site being disturbed.

"The Nabian and Sulux authorities have given their permission," Melody said. "Apparently, this is a new phase of cooperation amongst them and humans. You started something wonderful."

"It doesn't feel very wonderful," Belle said.

She stood and watched the activity for a while. When people started to recognize who Belle was, they pointed at her and tried to capture her holo-image. Two women approached her and began asking about how she found the site. That's when she decided it was time to head home.

"I assume you were referring to your friendship with Ta'al earlier," Melody said as she creaked along beside Belle. Her leg joints needed be lubricated. Belle had fallen behind on her duties in taking care of Melody. "I have been wondering where she is."

"She won't talk to me," Belle said. She kicked at the pebbles on the path. "I tried to call her, but her parents always say she's busy. I don't know what I did wrong."

Melody extended her arm high above their heads as they passed under a tall Martian apple tree. She plucked a fruit and gave it to Belle, who took a big bite. The juice dripped down her chin.

"From what I have learned of human relationships, I think it would work best to go to her house and speak to her in person," Melody said. "To get the story from the 'mouth of the horsel' — I believe that is the expression."

Belle looked sideways at her android and smiled. Both because of Melody's strange saying, and because she knew the android was right.

"That's a brilliant idea," she said. Then she hesitated. "What if Ta'al says she never wants to see me again?"

"I would think by now you should realize that life is about taking risks," Melody said. "If you do not try, you will not know."

Belle laughed. Her android was so wise. "Let's go!"

By the time they reached Ta'al's house, Belle was very thirsty. The apple had been juicy, but it was also sweet. She longed for a glass of water.

The Nabians' above-ground house was nicer than anyone else's in the area. They had rebuilt it from the ground up. The stone they used to build the house was red, like the rocky hills beyond the terraformed areas of Mars. The roof was flat and there was an extra section on top that looked like a cross between a doughnut and a space ship. The windows cut into the stone were triangular and made the house look like it had eyes.

Belle walked up to the computer panel by the door and pressed the doorbell button. When the panel lit up, she made sure her face was directly in front of the camera.

"I've come to see Ta'al," she said.

"Ta'al is . . . busy." It was Fa'erz who answered.

"I can wait," Belle said. She was determined to see her friend, even if it meant she had to wait outside all day. "Tell her I'll be sitting on the step, right here, until she can talk to me."

Belle heard Fa'erz say something in their language. Then the panel went dark again.

Belle sat down, and the sun beat down on her. It was a hot summer day on Mars. And Melody had not brought along any water. It was just more bad luck for Belle.

"Perhaps we can come back tomorrow," Melody suggested. "That way, you can get your water, and Ta'al will have more time to consider meeting you."

But Belle refused to budge. "I'll stay here until I die of thirst, if I have to."

"I believe that is an exaggeration," Melody said.

They sat in silence for a long time. Drops of sweat beaded on Belle's forehead. Even Melody started to feel hot to the touch. Then they heard a sound. The door was opening. Belle jumped up and turned to look. Sure enough, Ta'al was at the door.

"What do you want?" she asked. She sounded so sharp that Belle suddenly couldn't remember why she was there.

"I don't understand why you're so angry with me," Belle said after she gathered her thoughts. She walked up the steps to meet her friend. Ta'al stepped onto the porch as the door slid shut behind her.

"From what I can tell, the argument between your people and the Sulux and the Martians is being fixed," Belle said. "So . . . I don't know why you're so upset with me for falling into that shaft."

Ta'al tilted her head and frowned. "Is that what you think? That I'm mad at you for falling into a hole?"

Belle frowned and shrugged. Had she done something even worse to make Ta'al mad at her?

Ta'al crossed her arms over her chest and shook her head. It made Belle feel stupid.

"You'll have to tell me," Belle said. "Because I can't figure it out."

"Why aren't you with Ava today?" Ta'al said.

"Ava? Why would I be with Ava?" Belle asked, staring at Ta'al. She felt even more confused than before.

"Isn't she your new best friend?"

Oh! So that's what this is about, Belle thought to herself. She finally understood.

"You think Ava and I are best friends?" Belle said. "And that's why you're mad at me?"

"Well, the two of you seemed pretty friendly at the cave," Ta'al said. "And then you spent all your time with her at school. You even let her take my desk at class. What happened? Did she leave you for someone new? So now you have no one else to hang out with?"

Belle couldn't believe her ears. "Ta'al, after we were at the cave my parents grounded me. I was in my room alone for days. And since then we've been pestered by non-stop visitors and scientists. I've practically been hiding in my house to keep away from all of them. I haven't seen Ava in days, and . . . I really don't care to."

Ta'al glared at Belle for a long time, as if she was studying her face. "So she's not your best friend?"

"Oh my stars, no!" Belle smacked her forehead. "She's so full of herself and exhausting to be around. She never stops talking about herself, or how wonderful her life on Earth used to be."

"She does talk a lot about Earth." A hint of a smile played on Ta'al's lips. "She should realize that Mars is her new home now."

"Yeah. Earth is old news."

Ta'al giggled.

"Ta'al, I've missed you," Belle said, blinking fast to hold back the tears. "Can we please be friends again?"

Ta'al nodded and Belle threw herself at her friend. She wrapped her arms around Ta'al and gave her a huge bear hug.

"Gently!" Ta'al gasped. "You'll squeeze me to death."

Belle let go and laughed. Ta'al laughed too. It was the best moment Belle had had in days.

The girls sat on the steps and talked and talked. They caught each other up on what they'd been doing.

"I'm disappointed that we didn't win the science fair," Ta'al said.

"Not even a special mention," Belle grumbled. "But I'm still glad we got to do the work. I learned so much about Nabian technology."

"And with Lucas, you learned about turkens too."

"Yes, enough to last a lifetime," Belle chuckled.

"I am glad to see that you two are friends again," Melody said. She'd been so quiet during the last few minutes, Belle almost forgot she was there. "I believe what you have experienced is known as a misunderstanding."

Belle and Ta'al agreed.

"It reminds me of a joke," Melody continued. "A Martian asked an official how long it would take to fly to Earth. The official went to check the schedule, saying, 'Just a minute . . .' so the Martian said thank you and left."

The girls stared at Melody for several long seconds trying to understand the story.

"Oh, I see!" Ta'al exclaimed. "The Martian thought it only takes a minute to get to Earth. He misunderstood!"

Belle laughed and laughed, until her belly ached. Melody's eyes turned bright pink with pleasure.

"I'm just glad we're friends again," Belle said, drying her tears of laughter.

"Me too," Ta'al said. "It was so boring without you."

Belle got to her feet, and turned to face her friend. She put on a somber face.

"I only have one more serious question to ask you."

"What is it?" Ta'al sounded worried.

Belle took a deep breath. "I have to ask you . . . beg you, really . . . for a glass of water!"

Oh the relief! I have my best friend back.

Ta'al and I spent the rest of the day talking and exploring her family's farm. We dug up bugs, which I didn't really like. But she enjoys it, so I tried to like it. I tried some of the Nabian fruit they grow in their gardens too. It was delicious!

Later, we practiced throwing empty Petripuffs at posts. My aim is definitely getting better. I helped Ta'al with her chores, and we finished our homework too. We were so good that our parents agreed to let her come over to my house. We're having a matekap — a sleepover.

Just before we went to bed tonight, Mom made an announcement. She's decided to have a special Martian commemoration day for Thea tomorrow. It's a custom here, where they celebrate a baby's third month of life. Mom's invited all the neighbors to come.

Unfortunately, that means Ava will be coming too.

CHAPTER TEN

FRIENDS OLD
AND NEW

The next morning, Belle and Taal were put to
work. They had to clean the Songs' house, and then
help Zara make decorations for the party. They cut
out tiny stars from old packing boxes, painted them,
and strung them together.

"This would be so much easier if we used a 3D
printer," Belle complained. Her hands were sore from
cutting all the stars.

"I used to do this as a child with my friends," Zara said. "It's nice to use your hands once in a while."

"I'm actually enjoying this," Ta'al said. She was good at saying things that made parents like her. But Belle didn't mind. She was just happy to have Ta'al there.

After finishing the decorations, Belle worked on doing her chores while Ta'al followed, holding Thea in her arms. When they introduced the baby to the turkens, she squealed with delight. In Loki's stall, Thea stared wide-eyed at the giant creature. Belle wasn't sure if her baby sister should be near the huge horsel. But Loki was so gentle that Belle was quite surprised.

"He wasn't that nice to me when we first met," she said.

However, Raider turned out to be Thea's favorite. Belle held Thea up as she rode on the wolf-dog's back. Raider didn't seem to mind. He walked slowly and carefully around the yard, as if he understood that Thea was just a baby. She giggled and made all kinds of funny noises.

People began to arrive for the party exactly at teatime. The Walkers came first. They brought a huge gift-wrapped present for Thea. It had pretty bows on it and hand-drawn designs on the wrapping.

"It's my own artwork," Myra said proudly. "Even though the paper is the artificial stuff." Real paper was rare and expensive on Mars.

"We'll have to be extra careful when we open it then," Zara said. "I want to keep your lovely work."

Lucas volunteered to carry Thea for a while. He was surprisingly good at it.

"Maybe you should have a baby sister too," Belle said jokingly.

"It would be fun to have a sister — or a brother — to play with," he replied.

Thea rubbed his face with her tiny hands and laughed. Lucas laughed and didn't seem to mind. Thea did it for a whole ten minutes, until Ta'al's parents arrived.

"You'll be pleased to hear that a new organization has been formed," So'ark told everyone. "Terran, Martian, Sulux, and Nabian representatives will meet regularly to work through the difficulties we've had in the past. We will 'put it all on the table,' as the Terran expression goes."

"That sounds like a step in the right direction," Yun said. "There are a lot of questions to answer, especially for the human authorities. But I'm hopeful that all the races can leave the past behind and work together for a bright future here on Mars."

"How do you feel about it?" Zara asked Ta'al's parents, serving them a cup of Martian tea.

"Being adversaries with one's neighbors is taxing on the spirit," He'ern said. "I, for one, am open to this change."

Belle frowned and looked to Ta'al. She always had trouble understanding Ta'al's dad. He used such big words.

"He means, it's tiresome to be angry at your neighbors all the time," Ta'al whispered.

"You are so right," Myra said, smiling at Ta'al. "It's time we learned to live together in peace. Our own children have already shown us how."

Lucas came into the room with Thea in his arms. "Look what I taught her to do." He showed the baby his palm, and she met it with hers. "She high-fived me!"

That broke the serious atmosphere in the room. Everyone laughed. Lucas and Thea repeated their trick over and over to everyone's delight.

A few minutes later the main door swished open as the Senn family walked in.

Alex and Aiden came into the house first. They brought a small box with them and showed the contents to Lucas, Belle, and Ta'al. Lucas and Ta'al were fascinated by their collection of colorful insects. Belle only pretended to be interested in the bugs.

"We found these all around our farm," Aiden said.

"Do you know where all these bugs came from?" Alex added. "Can you believe they were accidentally brought from Earth in grain bags?"

Belle looked at Lucas and laughed. He'd told her the very same thing shortly after they had met.

Ava came in last, behind her parents.

"I don't want to go anywhere near those disgusting creatures," she said. "They're almost as bad as that horrid lizard Aiden caught in the cave."

She waved hello to Belle's and Lucas' parents, but completely ignored Ta'al and her family. Mr. and Mrs. Senn, though, seemed quite happy to talk to everyone.

Ava slipped her arm through Belle's, pulling her away from Ta'al. "Show me around your house, bestie! I want to see your room."

Belle looked over at Ta'al, who shrugged. Gently, Belle peeled Ava off of her and looked her straight in the eye. Her heart beat hard against her chest. This could go really badly, but it was time to be brave and stand up for her friend.

"Ava," Belle began quietly. "I'm really glad you've moved here to Sun City, and I like you." She didn't add 'some of the time' like she wanted to. That would've been rude. "But Ta'al is my best friend. If you don't like her, that'll make it hard for all of us to be friends."

Ava frowned and bit her lower lip. She glanced at Ta'al, then Lucas, and finally Belle. Ta'al came closer and offered her hand.

"I don't think we've spoken at all since you arrived," Ta'al said. "We can start again, if you want."

Ava pursed her lips. "It's just really hard to get used to how you look."

"*What?*" Ta'al and Belle said at the same time.

"I mean, your nose is on top of your face!" Ava exclaimed.

"Ava, that's rude!" Alex walked over to Ta'al's side. "You should apologize."

Ta'al shook her head. "At least she's honest."

Belle wasn't so sure this was the right response to Ava's outburst.

Ta'al stepped closer. "Not all Terrans have spent time with aliens, Nabian or otherwise," she said. "And we do take some getting used to."

"I didn't," Belle protested. "I liked you right away."

Ta'al smiled at her. "Be honest," she said. "My appearance did alarm you at first, though you hid it well."

Belle blushed. "Maybe just a little. And only for a very short time."

Ta'al turned to Ava. "Can you imagine how we Nabians felt when we first encountered humans? You look as strange to us as we do to you."

The crease between Ava's eyebrows deepened. She was silent for a long while. Then her frown broke into a smile.

"Oh my gosh! You're right!" She spoke so loudly, even the adults turned around to see what was going on. "I just realized it. To you, I'm an alien!" She threw her head back and laughed. Belle thought it was a bit too dramatic.

Ta'al's eyes, which usually reflected the colors of her surroundings, turned a bright blue and pink, the color of Ava's clothes. She burst into laughter too. Together, they were so loud that Belle was stunned for a second.

"It's true," Ta'al said, with tears of laughter in her eyes. "We're all aliens to each other . . . until we become friends."

Belle gave her best friend a sideways hug. She sounded so wise when she said things like that.

As more guests arrived, Belle and Ta'al helped Melody serve drinks and food.

"Can I help too?" Ava asked. "The boys are racing their bugs, and they make me squirm."

Belle and Ta'al were happy to let Ava join them. They cut up the giant cake that Melody had made, and served each guest a slice.

"Oh, my. Is this cake made from mealworm flour?" Myra Walker asked.

"It is indeed," Melody replied. "I made a small change to your recipe. Is it acceptable?"

"Oh, it's delicious," Myra said. "I didn't know mealworm flour could have such a smooth texture. You must tell me what you did." She followed Melody into the kitchen where the android showed her how to change the recipe.

"Melody is a wonderful addition to your family," Myra said, emerging from the kitchen. "I don't know why we were afraid of her when we first met."

"It just goes to show," Belle whispered to her friends, "that sometimes first impressions can be wrong." She was so glad her neighbors were warming to her android. Melody was her oldest friend and would never hurt anyone. She had saved Belle's life on many occasions, and her friends' lives too.

"All it takes is getting to know someone better," Ava added. She blushed when she said that, glancing at Ta'al. "New friends can bring great rewards."

"Well, I suppose everyone can learn to be more open about new friends," Ta'al said. Then she looked over at Raider, who was munching on a bone in the corner. She walked over to him and scratched him behind his chewed-up ear. "So, I suppose I can at least try to be less afraid of the dog."

Laughter filled the Song house. Even Thea giggled at every new stranger she met that day. Belle couldn't have been happier.

It had taken a whole year to get used to life on Mars, but Belle finally felt like this was truly home.

She couldn't wait to discover more adventures on the red planet. It could be dangerous, and she might get into trouble again. But with her android, her dog, and her growing group of friends, she knew she could handle whatever the future had in store.

Sol 102/Summer, Mars Cycle 106

This was the best day ever! The party went on all afternoon. We played games, and Lucas even helped Thea ride on Raider. She really seems to love pretending that our dog is a horse!

In the evening, we went upstairs to watch the stars come out. We brought chairs and picnic blankets and kept our eyes on the heavens. What a show it gave us! We spotted all kinds of constellations.

Then Dad introduced us to an old game that his dad had taught him as a kid. It's called hide-and-seek. I found the best place to hide, under a pile of hay in Loki's stables. No one found me, so I won the game. I think!

Thea surprised everyone by sitting up on the blanket all by herself. She's a fast learner, that one. I bet when she's old enough, we'll be going on adventures together. I wonder if she'll be as good at breaking rules as I am?

ABOUT THE AUTHOR

A.L. Collins learned a lot about writing from her teachers at Hamline University in St. Paul, MN. She has always loved reading science fiction stories about other worlds and strange aliens. She enjoys creating and writing about new worlds, as well as envisioning what the future might look like. Since writing the Redworld series, she has collected a map of Mars that hangs in her living room and a rotating model of the red planet, which sits on her desk. When not writing, Collins enjoys spending her spare time reading and playing board games with her family. She lives near Seattle, Washington with her husband and five dogs.

• • • ● ● • •

ABOUT THE ILLUSTRATOR

Tomislav Tikulin was born in Zagreb, Croatia. Tikulin has extensive experience creating digital artwork for book covers, posters, DVD jackets, and production illustrations. Tomislav especially enjoys illustrating tales of science fiction, fantasy, and scary stories. His work has also appeared in magazines such as *Fantasy & Science Fiction, Asimov's Science Fiction, Orson Scott Card's Intergalactic Medicine Show,* and *Analog Science Fiction & Fact.* Tomislav is also proud to say that his artwork has graced the covers of many books including Larry Niven's *The Ringworld Engineers,* Arthur C. Clarke's *Rendezvous With Rama,* and Ray Bradbury's *Dandelion Wine* (50th anniversary edition).

:WHAT DO YOU THINK?:

1. Belle and Ta'al are the best of friends, but a misunderstanding causes them to stop speaking to one another. What could Belle or Ta'al have done differently to avoid harming their friendship?

2. After the ancient Nabian site was discovered, the artifacts and relics were carefully removed and taken to a museum. Why do you think the scientists took the artifacts instead of leaving them in the cave?

3. When the kids were exploring the cave, Ta'al began to argue that the Nabians were on Mars first and that humans shouldn't have colonized the planet. Why do you think she feels this way? Do you agree or disagree with her opinion?

4. Pretend that you are in Belle's place when she falls into the deep, dark hole. How would you feel? What would you do? Write about how you would get yourself out of the hole or survive until you were rescued.

5. During much of the story, Belle thinks Ava is annoying and full of herself. What would you do if you had a friend like her? Write about what you could do to help that person be a better friend.

GLOSSARY

contaminate (kuhn-TA-muh-nayt)—to make dirty or unfit for use

coincidence (kih-IN-si-duhnss)—something that happens accidentally at the same time as something else

desecrate (DESS-uh-krayt)—to treat something or some place that is considered holy and sacred with disrespect

excavate (EK-skuh-vayt)—to dig in the earth to search for ancient remains or ruins

gait (GAYT)—the manner in which a horse moves

hologram (HOL-uh-ram)—an image made by laser beams that looks three-dimensional

jurisdiction (joor-is-DIK-shuhn)—legal authority to enforce the law in a certain area

perimeter (puh-RIM-uh-tur)—the outer edge or boundary of an area

prejudice (PREJ-uh-diss)—an opinion about others that is unfair and not based on facts

terraform (TER-uh-form)—to change the environment of a planet or moon to make it capable of supporting life

torso (TOR-soh)—the part of the body between the neck and waist, not including the arms

⋮MARS TERMS⋮

holo-vid (HOHL-uh-vid)—a holographic projection that shows videos for information or entertainment

horsel (HOHRSS-el)—a hybrid animal that is part horse and part camel, used as a work animal on Mars

Mars Cycle (MARS SY-kuhl)—the Martian year, equal to 687 Earth days, or 1.9 Earth years

matekap (MAH-teh-kap)—Nabian word meaning "sleepover"

Nablan (NAY-bee-uhn)—an advanced alien race with nose ridges and plastic-like hair; their eye color reflects their surroundings

para-ta-num-peia (PAIR-uh-tah-noom-PAY-uh)—Nabian phrase meaning "no-man's land"

Protector (proh-TEK-tohr)—a large black robot that works to enforce the laws of Mars

Sol (SOHL)—the name for the Martian day

Sulux (SUH-lux)—an alien race with purple skin and arm and neck ridges

Terran (TAIR-uhn)—a person or thing that is originally from Earth

turken (TUR-ken)—a hybrid bird that is part turkey and part chicken; farmers on Mars raise them for their eggs and meat

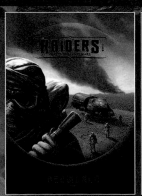